Jonathan Swift, author of Gulliver's Travels, *was born in Dublin in 1667 but spent a good deal of his life in England. He was an ordained priest but was extremely active in politics and was also a close friend of other well-known writers of that period such as Addison and Steele.*

For over 250 years, people everywhere have enjoyed reading about Lemuel Gulliver's travels in the strange countries of Lilliput and Brobdingnag. The tiny people of Lilliput are so fascinating that the word 'Lilliputian' is now part of the English language. Although this famous tale was originally written as a political satire, its instant appeal to all ages has been as a story.

The people of Lilliput, with their curiously human failings, and the people of Brobdingnag, who are so much larger than life, are vividly portrayed by Martin Aitchison.

Revised edition

© LADYBIRD BOOKS LTD MCMLXXVII

GULLIVER'S TRAVELS

Jonathan Swift

retold in simple language
by Marie Stuart

with illustrations by Martin Aitchison

Ladybird Books Loughborough

A Journey to Lilliput

When I was quite young, I had been sent to college to learn to be a doctor. Unhappily, my training was more than my father could afford. I had to leave and I became an apprentice to a famous surgeon in London. I stayed with him for four years and then went to Holland to study medicine.

While I was studying I spent what little spare money I had on learning navigation and mathematics, for I was keen to travel.

On my return from Holland, I had the chance of my first voyage as a ship's doctor. In the next few years I sailed to many strange lands aboard the *Swallow*.

When I came back, I decided to settle down in London and there got married. For several years I tried to earn my living as a doctor in London but finally had to go back to sea again. On a series of voyages to the East and West Indies I did however manage to add to my fortune. I also spent my time ashore studying the people and their language.

The last of these voyages was not very successful and I decided, once again, to try to earn a living ashore. I moved, with my wife and family, to the East End of London, hoping to find work amongst the sailors. For three years I worked hard to build up a practice, but could not earn the money I needed to support my family.

At about this time I met Captain Pritchard of the *Antelope*. He told me of his next voyage to the South Seas and offered me a place as ship's doctor. To this I readily agreed and having said goodbye to my wife and two children, we set sail from Bristol on May 4th 1699.

All went well for the first few weeks. Then there was a bad storm and the ship was wrecked. Six of the crew, of whom I was one, got into a little boat and began to row to an island nearby. Suddenly a huge wave upset the boat, and all the other men were lost. Only I, Lemuel Gulliver, was left.

I swam as long as I could and at last, just as I could swim no more, my feet touched the bottom. I waded through the water to the shore, where there was no sign of houses or people.

I walked about half a mile further, but still saw no one. Tired out, I lay down on the short, soft grass and went to sleep.

When I woke up it was daylight. I lay still for a moment wondering where I was, then tried to get up. I could not move my arms or my legs or my head! I was tied to the ground!

Suddenly I felt something moving on my left leg. It walked up me and stopped close by my chin. I looked down as well as I could (for my hair was tied to the ground), and saw a tiny man, less than six inches high, with a bow and arrow in his hand. Then many more of these little men started to run all over me. I was so surprised that I roared loudly. They ran back in a fright and fell over one another trying to get away.

I managed to break the strings that tied my left arm to the ground, and pulled some of my hair loose so that I could move my head. This made the little men even more afraid, and they shot arrows at me.

The little men stood around at a distance watching me. After a while, when they saw I was not going to hurt them, they cut some of the strings that bound me.

Now I could see that they had built a little platform beside my head so that their emperor could talk to me. He spoke for some time, but I could not understand him, and I began to grow hungry. I pointed to my mouth and pretended to chew. He at once sent some of his men to bring me food and drink.

Ladders were put against my sides, and over a hundred of the little men climbed up, bringing

6

baskets full of meat and bread. Each piece of meat was the size of one small piece of mince, so I had to keep asking for more. The loaves were so tiny that I ate three at a time.

I drank a whole barrel of their wine at a gulp. They kept looking at each other as if they could not believe it was possible to drink so much, but they brought me some more.

I made signs to let them know I would not try to escape, and they loosened the strings so that I could turn on my side. They also put some ointment on my face and hands, which took away the soreness their arrows had caused. Then I fell asleep again.

Whilst I was asleep, the emperor had decided
to move me to the capital city. This could only be
done by using the sort of cart they used to move
their ships from the woods to the sea. Being good
mathematicians, they had worked out a system of
pulleys and hoists that could lift me onto the cart.

Even so, it took five hundred carpenters to make
the cart and nine hundred men to work the pulleys
before I was safely tied down.

When I woke up I found myself on a kind of platform with wheels. It was moving towards the main city of these tiny people about half a mile away. Fifteen hundred of the emperor's largest horses, each about as big as my hand, were pulling me along.

For some time I did not know what had wakened me. I was told later however that some of the young people wanted to see how I looked when I was asleep. They climbed onto the platform and walked very softly up to my face. One of them, an officer in the Guards, put the sharp end of his spear up into my nose, which tickled my nose like a straw and made me sneeze, waking me up. They ran away quickly before I caught sight of them.

We made a long march for the remainder of that day and rested at night. They put five hundred guards on each side of me ready to shoot me if I tried to escape.

At last we arrived at the capital city. The platform to which I was tied stopped outside a church which was no longer used. Since this was the largest building in the whole country, the emperor had planned that I should live there. The door was just big enough for me to creep through when I wanted to sleep. Once inside, I could only lie down.

The little men would not let me go free, however. They put nearly a hundred of their tiny chains round my left leg, so that although I could stand up, I could not move very far.

When this was done, the emperor came to see me. He carried in his hand a sword about as big as one of our darning needles, to defend himself if I should break loose. He was a handsome little man, much taller than the rest of his court, who were with him, and he wore a gold helmet with a plume on the crest. All the ladies and gentlemen of the court were dressed in gold and silver.

I tried to answer the emperor when he spoke to me, but he could not understand any of the many languages which I speak. Soon he went away to decide whether he would have me killed or not, for I would cost a great deal to feed, and might be dangerous.

After the emperor had gone away, a great crowd of the tiny people came to see me. Some of the men shot arrows at me, and one just missed my eye.

The guards tied these men up and gave them to me to punish.

I put five of them in my pocket, and pretended I was going to eat the other one, who was very frightened. Then I took out my penknife and cut the cords that bound him, and set him on the ground. I treated the other five in the same way, taking them one by one out of my pocket. Everyone was very surprised to see me treat them so gently.

Two of the guards went to the emperor to tell him what I had done. He decided that since I had been kind to his people, he would not have me killed. He ordered people who lived close to the town to bring me six cows and forty sheep every day, and wine to drink. This was only just enough for me, since everything was so tiny.

Three hundred tailors were told to make clothes for me, and six hundred of the little people were to look after me. They were to live in tents outside the church to make it easier for them.

As the news of my arrival spread through the land, more and more people came to see me. Farmhands and housewives stopped what they were doing and, for a time, little work was done. In the end, the emperor proclaimed that those that had already seen me must go home. Only those who had a special licence from the court could come within fifty yards of my house. This did not apply to the emperor's troops, who were ordered to parade in front of me, so that the men and horses could get used to me.

There still remained the biggest problem: I could not understand them and they could not understand me. So the emperor sent six of his greatest scholars to teach me their language.

Three weeks later I was able to understand and talk to the little men. The first thing I asked the emperor was to set me free. He said that they must first see if I was carrying anything that could be a danger to his people. Two men came to look through my pockets, and wrote down everything they found.

They gave me a new name: the Great Man Mountain. In my pockets they found:

A handkerchief which they thought was like a carpet.

A snuff box which they called a chest filled with dust. It made them sneeze.

A notebook in which they recognised very large writing.

A comb. They knew what this was for, but said it looked like the railings round the emperor's palace.

A knife, a razor, and a pair of pistols. All these things were new to them, and they could not think what they were for.

A watch. They said it made a noise like a water-mill.

A purse. They called this a net large enough for a fisherman, but they knew I used it as a purse.

When the two little men had finished looking in my pockets, they looked at my belt. They wrote down that I had a sword as long as five men and a pouch with two pockets. One of these pockets held black powder, the other very heavy round balls.

They took their list to the emperor, who asked me to take out my sword and put it carefully on the ground. Then he asked me what my pistols were for. I told him not to be afraid, and I fired one of them in the air.

Everyone fell down in fright except the emperor, although he too went very white. He made me give up my pistols at once.

All my things were put away in the emperor's store room, except for my eye-glasses which were in a pocket the men had not found.

Slowly the emperor and his people came to understand that they were in no danger from me. From time to time some of them would dance on my hand, and the boys and girls liked to play hide and seek in my hair as I lay on the ground.

On one occasion the emperor asked me to stand with my legs apart so that his army could march between them. There were no less than 3,000 foot soldiers twenty-four abreast and 1,000 horsemen in columns sixteen abreast.

The horsemen in particular enjoyed using me as an obstacle. They would jump over my hand as it lay on the ground.

This skill and agility is common amongst the people. Nowhere is it better shown than in the selection of candidates for important posts. These men perform balancing acts on a rope. The one who jumps highest without falling off, gets the job. Often, the chief ministers have to show their skill. Flimnap, the Treasurer, has been known to do several somersaults on a rope one inch further off the ground than anyone else.

I was told that it was not uncommon for the performers to hurt themselves and even to break a limb. Each minister is trying so hard to show how much cleverer he is than his colleagues, that he will attempt things that are beyond his powers.

A year or two before my arrival, Flimnap had just such an accident. If it had not been for one of the king's cushions, lying conveniently on the floor, he would undoubtedly have broken his neck.

One day some people came to tell the emperor that they had found a huge black object lying on the ground. They said it was not alive, and they thought it might belong to the Great Man Mountain. It was my hat, which I thought I had lost at sea! To bring it to me, they made two holes in the brim and fastened cords from the hat to the harnesses of five horses.

I asked
once more to
be set free, and
at last the emperor
agreed, so long as I
would obey his rules.

I had always wanted to see the capital city, and
now that I was free the emperor said I could. All
the people were told to stay in their houses in case I
walked on them. So they crowded to their windows
to see me as I stepped over the wall into the square
where the emperor's palace stood.

It was really magnificent, like a big doll's house.
I lay down to look inside and the empress came to
the window, smiling, and gave me her hand to kiss.

19

Soon after I was set free, one of the country's great men came to see me. We had a long talk and I learned many things.

"You may have seen," he said, "that some of us wear high heels and some wear low heels on our shoes. The emperor will let only people wearing low heels work for him, and those who like high heels feel that this is wrong. Because of this there are many quarrels."

Then he told me of a much bigger danger that was about to befall his country.

"There is an island close by called Blefuscu, and the people there are going to attack us."

"Why?" I asked him.

"It all began long ago," he replied. "When our emperor's great-grandfather was a little boy, he cut his finger one morning as he took the top off his egg. Up till then everyone had cut off the big end of the egg. After that, however, the ruler of those times said that everyone must cut off the small end, and those who would not obey had to leave Lilliput.

"They went to the island of Blefuscu and called themselves the Big-Endians.

"This law about which end of the egg you should cut has caused a great deal of trouble. Many of our people preferred to die rather than obey it.

The rulers of Blefuscu have always supported the Big-Endians.

"So any Big-Endians in Lilliput who felt they were in danger, escaped to Blefuscu. Over the years there have been constant battles. Each side has lost many of its finest ships and thousands of men. Now we have found out that Blefuscu is preparing to invade us with a great fleet of ships. The emperor wants you to help us."

"Tell the emperor that I do not want to take sides in the argument, but I will help the people of Lilliput in any way I can."

I looked across to the island of Blefuscu and listened to the reports of the Lilliput scouts. By this means, I knew that the Big-Endian fleet of about fifty warships lay at anchor and I planned to seize them.

My plan was this: I fixed fifty hooks to fifty lengths of cord so that I could attach one to each of their ships. There was only about half a mile of sea between the islands, and I could wade most of the way. Right in the middle I had to swim for a short distance.

After half an hour I was close to their fleet. The sailors were so frightened by my size that they all jumped overboard and swam ashore, joining the

many thousands who were watching. I then set about fastening a hook to the prow of each ship.

Whilst I was busy with the hooks and cords, the Big-Endians fired thousands of their tiny arrows at me. These made me smart and were a great nuisance. In particular, I was afraid one might go in my eye. I remembered my glasses that I had kept in a secret pocket, and quickly put them on. They protected me and allowed me to get on with my work. Having made sure all the ships were firmly attached, I tied the ends of the cords together. Then I started to pull, but nothing happened! Of course, every ship was held fast by its anchor and I had to cut each anchor cable.

Taking the knotted cord in my hand, I started to wade back to Lilliput. The people of Blefuscu were astonished. They had seen me cut the anchor ropes

and probably thought that I would just let the ships float away. When they saw their whole fleet being towed away, they screamed and shouted in rage and despair. Once I was out of range of their arrows, I stopped to pull out the ones that had stuck in my hands and face and to put on some soothing ointment. I took off my glasses and once more headed for Lilliput.

Meanwhile, the emperor and all his court stood waiting on the shore. The first sight they saw was a group of ships coming steadily towards them. They could not see me, because I was chest deep in the water. As I reached the deeper part of the channel their fears grew, for it was here I had to swim; only my head was above water. The emperor was afraid I had been drowned and that the ships were coming to invade him after all.

Soon the channel grew shallower and they were relieved to see me holding the end of the cords that pulled the ships. When they could hear me, I shouted, "Long live the emperor of Lilliput!" and held up the tow-rope. The emperor was so pleased with me that he made me a Nardac, which is something like a duke in my own country. Now the emperor wanted me to seize the rest of the enemy's ships, so that he could be emperor of the Big-Endians as well as Lilliput. I would not do this as I did not think it was right.

This made the emperor angry with me.

Soon after this, some of the Big-Endians came to make peace with the Lilliputians. When they saw me again, they asked me to come to Blefuscu one day so that everyone could see how big I was. I said that I would, which made the emperor even more angry with me.

His Chief Admiral was displeased with me too, not only because it was I who had defeated the Big-Endian navy, but also because I had been made a Nardac.

There were others amongst the emperor's great men who did not like me. They all asked the emperor to have me put to death, as an enemy of Lilliput, because I had refused to do what the emperor wanted.

After a great deal of discussion and argument, the emperor decided not to have me put to death because of all the help I had given him. He agreed with the suggestion that I should be blinded and then later starved to death. There had been other ideas of setting fire to my house at night, of putting poison on my clothes and shooting me with arrows dipped in poison, but all these the emperor had turned down.

Naturally, all these discussions took place in great secrecy. It was only through the kindness of one of the important men at court that I was warned of my danger. This man came in secret late one night. He arrived in a sedan chair and immediately sent the chairmen away. I took the chair with the man in it, into my house and there he told me of all that had taken place in the council.

He left as secretly as he had come and I decided that the time had come for me to leave Lilliput. I did not like the thought of being blinded!

Having made up my mind, I quickly wrote to the secretary saying that I was leaving that morning for Blefuscu. I had, after all, got permission from the emperor to go.

On the far side of the island lay the fleet. I seized a large warship and soon had a cord tied to the prow. I took off my clothes and put them carefully in the ship so that they would not get wet.

29

Towing the ship behind me, I waded and swam across to the main port of Blefuscu. Many people greeted me and two of them agreed to guide me to the capital city. Here, I sent a message to the emperor, telling him of my arrival.

About an hour later, the messenger returned to say that the emperor and all his family with the chief ministers were coming out to receive me. When they arrived, they did not seem at all scared and I lay down carefully so that I could kiss their hands.

I explained that I had come as I had promised, with the full permission of the emperor of Lilliput, and that I would do anything I could to help him. I did not mention the trouble I had been in, for I did not see how he could find out.

Unknown to me, one of the Lilliput ministers had arrived, demanding that I should be sent back, bound hand and foot, to be punished as a traitor. The emperor of Blefuscu replied that this was not possible and anyway I had helped him a great deal. The emperor himself then asked me to stay, but I no longer trusted emperors and told him that I would like to go home.

This was to happen sooner than I had dared hope. Walking along the cliffs one day I suddenly saw a full size boat, floating upside down. I ran down to the shore and waded out, but it was too large and too far out for me to reach. I went back at once to the city to ask the emperor for help. He lent me all the ships that were left of his fleet, and all the seamen to man them. Whilst the fleet sailed round the island, I went overland to where I had last seen the boat.

The tide had brought it nearer the shore, so I swam out to it. The water was too deep for me to stand, so I swam behind and pushed, whilst nine ships towed in front. By this means we finally got the boat to the shore. In spite of having been adrift for some time, it did not seem to have come to any great harm.

It took two thousand of the tiny men to help me to turn the boat right side up once it was ashore. Then I had to get it ready for the long journey home.

The thickest linen these people had was much thinner than that of our finest handkerchiefs, so two sails were made for me by putting thirteen thicknesses together. Five hundred workmen were needed to make them!

When all was ready, I stored food on board, and also live cows and bulls and sheep which I wanted to show my family. Off I set, and two days later I saw a big ship, whose captain took me on board. He did not believe my story until he saw the live cows and bulls and sheep, which were in my pocket.

When at last I got home, my wife and children were very happy to see me again and to hear all my adventures. As for the cows and bulls and sheep, I put them to eat grass in a park close by my house, at Greenwich in London. Maybe you could see some of them there today if you went to look!

A JOURNEY TO Brobdingnag

After I had been at home for a while, I went to sea again, for I like to travel.

The first part of our voyage was pleasant, with nothing to trouble us. Then one day there was a bad storm, and we were driven hundreds of miles out of our way. We were lost. There was plenty of food on board, but not nearly enough water. So when one day we saw land, the captain sent several of us ashore to get water.

When we landed, there was no sign of a river or spring. The other men kept to the shore, looking for water near the sea. I walked inland, but I found no water and turned back.

From where I stood, I could see our ship's boat with all the men on board, rowing as quickly as they could back to the ship. They had left me behind! Then I saw why. There was a huge man-like creature chasing them, taking great strides through the sea.

I did not wait to see what happened. I ran away as fast as I could, and climbed a steep hill to see what the country looked like.

I learnt afterwards that the giant that was chasing the boat had given up. In his haste, he had not seen the sharp rocks that were under the water and had stubbed his toe. The pain was so great that he stopped to nurse his injured foot and this allowed the sailors to escape.

When I got to the top of the hill, everything looked very strange.

I could not believe my eyes! The grass was nearly as tall as a house, with corn towering above it as high as a church steeple!

I walked along what I thought was a high road, but which I found out later was just a footpath to the people of this land, and I came to a stile.

Each step in this stile was like a high wall to me, and I could not climb it. As I was looking for a gap in the huge hedge, I saw another enormous man like the one I had seen chasing my friends. I was very frightened, and ran to hide in the corn.

This man was clearly in charge. When he called out, in a voice which sounded to me like thunder, seven other giants came towards him. They carried sickles, each as big as six of our own scythes, and were set to work to reap the corn.

As they moved forward, I moved back, to keep
out of the way of their cruel blades. The time came,
however, when I could not fight my way through
the tangle of stems. I thought of how a man from
Lilliput would feel in my own country. And I
remembered how easy it had been to pull a whole
fleet along with one hand. Now I was in a very
different situation. It occurred to me that these
huge men might think of me as a nice little snack.

I grew even more frightened. Where could I hide?
I ran to and fro to keep out of their way, but they
moved too fast for me to escape.

At last I called out "Stop!" as loudly as I could,

just as one was about to step on me. The man
looked down and picked me up, holding me tightly
in case I should bite him. Then he took me to his
master to show him what he had found.

This man was a farmer, and the same man I had
seen at first in the field.

The farmer pulled out his handkerchief, wrapped
me in it, and took me back to his farm. His wife
screamed and ran away when she first saw me, just
as my wife does when she sees a mouse!

Then the three children came to have a look at
me. They were just going to have their dinner, and
they put me on the table where they could see me as
they ate.

The farmer's wife gave me some crumbs of bread, and minced up some meat for me.

Then in came the nurse with the baby in her arms. He wanted me as a plaything. When they gave me to him, he put my head in his mouth.

I roared so loudly that the baby was frightened and dropped me. I would have been killed if his mother had not caught me in her apron.

After dinner the farmer went back to his fields, and his wife put me to bed with a handkerchief over me for a sheet.

Later on, the daughter of the house made a bed for me in the baby's cradle. This girl was very good to me. She was nine years old and small for her age in that country, since she was only forty feet tall!

She called me Grildrig, which meant "Little Man", and taught me to speak their language. I liked her very much.

As soon as the people who lived round about heard of me, they all came to have a look at me.

One of them told the farmer that he should take me to town next market day, and make people pay to see me. So he did this. His little girl came with us to look after me, and I called her my nurse.

I was placed on a table in the largest room of the inn, which was as big as a football field! I did all the funny tricks I could think of: stood on my head, hopped about, and danced, to please the people who came to see me.

The farmer made a great deal of money from showing me, and he decided to take me to other towns. At last we came to the capital city, where the royal family lived. Now we had been travelling for nearly ten weeks. Every day I had worked for at least eight hours, doing tricks for the people who came to see me.

Being in the capital city, my fame soon reached the ears of the queen. We were summoned to entertain her at court and as soon as she saw me, she wanted to buy me.

My master was glad to exchange me for a bag of gold and his daughter was allowed to stay to look after me. I was so pleased at this arrangement that I kissed the tip of the queen's finger in gratitude.

The queen was so delighted with me that she took me to the king. I explained as well as I could how I came to be in his country, but the phrases I had learnt from the farmer were not very suitable for use at court, and the king was still very puzzled.

His majesty then sent for three wise scholars to
decide what I was. After much argument, they
finally agreed that I was just a natural oddity.
At this point I asked permission to tell of my own
country, where millions like me lived.

At first they did not believe me, but I convinced
them in the end. The king then decided I was
something rather special, and should be looked after
with great care.

I always had my meals at a little table on the queen's table, now, but I did not like to see the way she ate. She would put a piece of bread as big as two of our loaves in her mouth at one go! Her dinner knife was taller than me, and I thought it looked very dangerous.

This was frightening enough, but one day my nurse took me to see some of the people at court eating. There I saw a dozen or more of these huge knives raised at the same time.

This was quite terrifying and looked to me more like the start of a battle than the beginning of a meal.

45

The queen had a little room made for me, with a roof that lifted up, and furniture which was just the right size for me. The queen had a set of silver cups, saucers and plates made for me, too. It was like a doll's tea-set to her!

Thinking of the trouble I might have with their small animals, which were to me like large dogs, I asked for a lock on my door.

46

The smallest the smith could make would have done well for the gates of a mansion in my own country.

Every Wednesday, which was their Sunday, the king came to have dinner with me. He liked to talk to me and to ask me about England. He wanted to find out in what ways we were different from the people in his own country of Brobdingnag.

When I had finished telling him all I could about our ways and customs, he decided that our two peoples were really very alike, except for size.

The only one I did not get on well with was the queen's dwarf. He was five times as tall as me — about thirty feet — but this was small for them. The king was twice as tall as he was!

The dwarf used to play tricks on me because the queen liked me better than him. Once he dropped me in a bowl of cream. I swam to the side and my nurse got me out.

I was pleased when they made a little boat for me and put it in a tub of water so that I could row about. Sometimes they put a sail on the boat. Then the queen and her women would make a wind for me with their fans.

Sometimes however life in Brobdingnag was no fun at all! Once I had to fight off some big wasps with my sword.

On another day, a monkey came into my room, and picked me up. I think he took me for a baby monkey, for he stroked my face gently as he held me. Suddenly there was a noise at the door, and he leaped through the window and up to the roof, carrying me with him.

They had to get ladders and climb up to drive the monkey away and bring me down.

The king was very interested in music and often arranged for concerts to be held at court. My box would be carried to the room so that I could hear, but this was no pleasure to me because of the loudness of the noise. If I had my box put at the far side of the room, closed my windows and door, and drew the curtains, the sound was just bearable.

My interest in music took a different form one day. My nurse was learning to play the spinet, and I decided I would entertain the king and queen by playing an English tune on it.

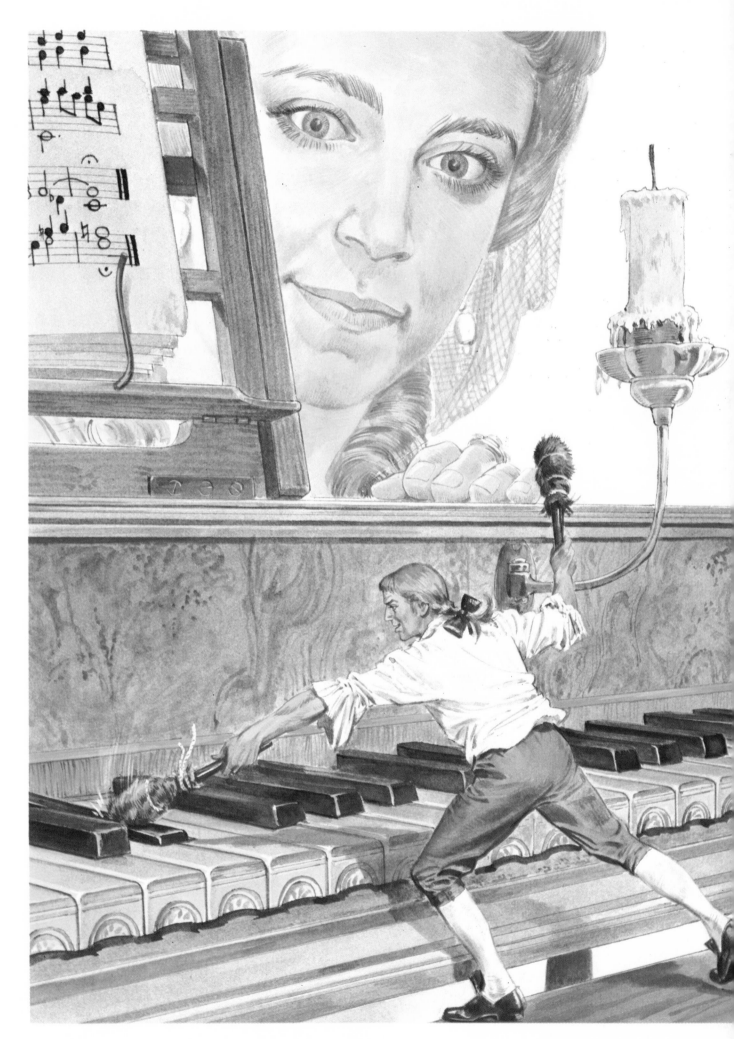

This was not easy, for the keys were a foot wide and the keyboard sixty feet long. However, I made two clubs and covered them with soft material, so as not to damage the keys. With these, I ran up and down a bench, striking the notes as I went by.

After our earlier talks, the king had become very interested in the affairs of my country. He had my box brought into his room, put on a table so that I was on a level with his head, and asked me to bring out one of my chairs to sit on. In this way we held long discussions about methods of government, the making of laws and the education of those who govern. The king was very critical of some of our systems and I determined to find a way of impressing him with our superior knowledge.

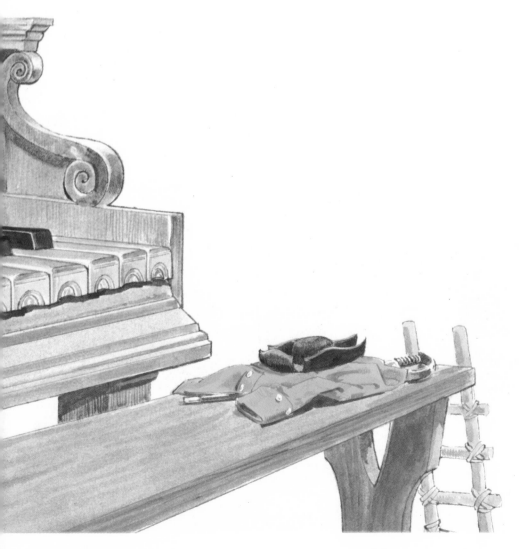

When the king was talking to me one day, I said I could teach him how to make gunpowder so that he would win a lot of wars. The king of Brobdingnag however was a very wise man. He said that he did not want to learn how to do it, and I must never talk about it again. He said that if a man could make two ears of corn, or two blades of grass, grow where only one grew before, he would do more good than he could ever do by winning a war.

Soon after this the king and queen and their servants set off on a long journey to another part of Brobdingnag. I went with them in my box. They fixed up a hammock in it so that I should not feel the bumps so much.

My nurse came too, but she caught a bad cold on the way. When at last we came to a stop, she had to rest in bed for a few days.

I knew we were near the sea, and I longed to see it again. Since my nurse was in bed, one of the queen's pages was told to take my box down to the sea shore. He went off to look for birds' eggs, and I fell asleep.

I awoke suddenly with a jolt. There was a loud swishing noise above me, and my box seemed to be moving upwards very fast. Then I guessed what had happened. A big bird, perhaps an eagle, had swooped down and picked up the ring of my box in his beak. I was flying through the air!

Soon there came a loud squawking, as if the eagle was fighting, and all at once I was falling. My box stopped with a great SPLASH! I was at sea!

Taking out my handkerchief, I tied it to my walking-stick. Then I stood on a chair and pushed my flag through the little trap-door, waving it to and fro and calling for help. No one came. I gave myself up for lost.

I sat without hope for a long time. Then, as I stared through the window, I suddenly realised that my box was being pulled along. Once more I pushed my flag out of the trap-door and called for help.

This time, to my great joy, someone answered —
in English! I begged him to come and let me out.

It was an English ship, with English sailors — not
giants, not little men, but people the same size as me!

At first the captain thought I had been shut up in
the box because I had done something very bad.
When I told him about the Brobdingnagians, he did
not believe me.

I showed him a gold ring the queen had given me —

I wore it round my neck like a collar. And I gave him a
giant's tooth which a dentist had taken out by mistake.

At last he believed me. He said he would take me
back to England with him, and we set sail for home.

Many weeks later, when I left the ship and came
on land again, the houses and people all looked so
small that I thought I must be in Lilliput once more.
When my wife heard all about the danger I had been
through, she said I must never go to sea again.

BROBD

Jonathan Swift 1667~1745

LILLIPUT